AROUND THE CARIBBEAN

Stories by
NORA BURGLON
THELMA GLAZER
E. MARK PHILLIPS

Illustrated by ANN ESHNER

D. C. HEATH AND COMPANY
BOSTON

Copyright, 1941, by D. C. Heath and Company
Printed in the U. S. A.

D. C. HEATH AND COMPANY
BOSTON · NEW YORK · CHICAGO · ATLANTA
SAN FRANCISCO · DALLAS · LONDON

NEW WORLD  NEIGHBORS

From the southern tip of Florida to the mouth of the Orinoco River in northeastern Venezuela, there is a string of islands, large and small, which enclose a famous sea. The islands are the West Indies and the sea is the Caribbean. Both the islands and the sea occupy a prominent place in the history of the New World. They are, in fact, the oldest part of our three Americas. Columbus, the Admiral of the Indies, was the first great sailor to explore this area.

One hundred years before the Pilgrims landed on the bare rock of Plymouth, there were famous churches and wealthy cities built by white men along the shores of the Caribbean, not only on the islands, but in Mexico, Central America, Colombia, and Venezuela. This region was the Spanish Main.

As you read AROUND THE CARIBBEAN, you will get better acquainted with the New World neighbors who live in this interesting part of our Americas today. When you come to know them better, you will find that they are not very different from the other Americans. Sugar, coffee, bananas, and mahogany are not the only things that they are capable of producing. Some very interesting people have been born in that part of America, including Alexander Hamilton, one of the founders of our own country.

—Dr. José Padín
Formerly Commissioner of Education
Puerto Rico

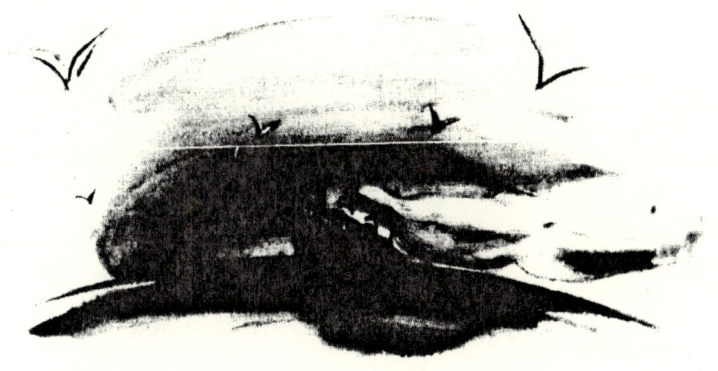

CONTENTS

DOUBLE DOORS . . . . Nora Burglon

A story of Cuba

Page 7

A KNIFE FOR PEDRO . . Thelma Glazer

A story of Colombia

Page 19

YOUNG BALSAMERO . . E. Mark Phillips

A story of El Salvador

Page 35

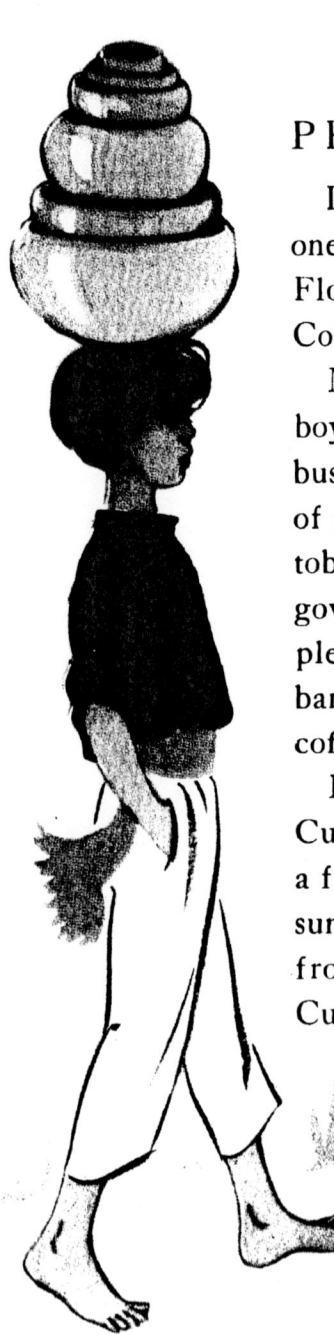

PRODUCTS OF CUBA

Diego lives in Cuba, an island about one hundred and fifty miles south of Florida. Cuba was discovered by Columbus on his first voyage in 1492.

Most of the people in Cuba, even boys like Diego, work in the sugar business. Cuba raises great quantities of sugar cane. It is also famous for its tobacco. In recent years the Cuban government has encouraged the people to raise other things such as bananas, pineapples, onions, *cacao* and coffee.

Living can be very pleasant in Cuba. It is a sub-tropical country with a fairly constant temperature. Even in summer there are breezes. Tourists from the United States like to go to Cuba for their vacations.

DOUBLE DOORS

BY NORA BURGLON

Diego was on his way to the village. He was walking with his back straight and his head in the air. He had to walk carefully because he was carrying clay pots on his head.

As he walked along, the sugar cane on one side of the road rustled softly as the wind blew through the leaves. On the other side of the road, the banana plants nodded and beckoned as though they had something to say to the boy.

Diego did not look their way, however. It was not necessary. He had helped with the planting of both the sugar cane and the banana plants and wanted nothing more to do with the plantations, for he hated the work.

Soon the time would come for the harvesting of the sugar cane. Diego was wondering if it would be possible to think up some good reason for working at the potter's wheel instead of cutting sugar cane with the heavy *machete*. The knife was almost as long as he. Cutting sugar cane with that heavy thing from morning until night was nothing to look forward to with any feeling of happiness.

Diego was wishing that the harvest season would never come. For a whole week now, he had been allowed to work at his father's potter's wheel. The pots he was carrying upon his head today he had made himself.

Many clay pots made by Cuban workmen were plain. Diego's father, however, had been a famous potter. He had always decorated his jars with designs made by painting them with clay of many colors.

The boy chuckled to himself. He had not told his mother that he had made these pots. Imagine how surprised she would be if he could sell them! Perhaps she would allow him to make pottery after that, instead of doing the hated work on the plantation.

"I hate bananas and sugar cane and pineapples," said Diego, as he walked along. "The bananas and pineapples are good to eat, but the work is too much. If only I could be a potter, instead!" Diego looked at the waving sugar cane and remembered the hard work of planting.

In the spring, furrows seven feet apart had been plowed the length of the field. Into these, sections of sugar cane had been dropped. They had been laid so closely they touched and, sometimes, even overlapped. Once planted they were covered with soil. In a few days, green shoots appeared at each joint of the cane. These became the sugar cane now standing beside the road, nodding and waving so prettily. Diego did not think about how pretty they were, but about how much work there would be in days to come when he would have to help strip them of tassels and leaves.

On the other side of the road were the banana plants. It had been Diego's job to set out the suckers, or shoots, which had sprung up from the roots of the old banana stumps. That was because the planter must have another field.

"More hot and sticky work," the boy grumbled. He was wondering if the day would ever come when he might work at the potter's wheel as long as he liked.

Before long Diego passed another field. It appeared to be covered with a low-growing cactus in whose heart a red-and-yellow blossom grew. Diego had worked in this field, too. He knew it was pineapple and not cactus at all. He had helped cut the suckers loose from the base of the parent pineapple plant and then set them out here.

Before Diego reached the village, many ox-carts rumbled by bringing in sugar cane, pineapples and bananas from the plantations. Some loads were to be shipped to the mills, others to the packers. The sugar cane was on the way to the mill, where the stalks would be crushed and rolled, to press out the sweet juice, and where the juice would later be boiled down into molasses, syrup, or refined into sugar.

Diego had once visited the sugar mill. He would never have believed, if he had not seen it himself, that fine white sugar could come out of the mess which had been mixed and boiled together. When the juice was squeezed out of the sugar cane, not only was lime added to it, but sulphur gas was forced through it. After much washing and whirling in cylinders, the mixture was bleached and became white sugar.

Diego thought of all these things as he walked steadily along the road to market. He had been curious and interested to see what happened to Cuba's sugar cane before it went out into the world. But he did not think his own part in the work was interesting.

When he arrived at the market, Diego found it a lively place. All about him were men and women displaying their goods in booths or upon the ground. More were coming every minute, carrying upon their heads baskets of fruit or nuts, fish or fowl, to be sold in the market.

Diego proudly arranged his clay pots upon the stone flags of the street. He was certain some northern visitor would be glad to buy them as gifts to send home to the United States.

A few booths away from him was a man with tiny clay pots which he had made. The pots were all of the same shape and each one held a small cactus plant. The pots were clumsy and very badly made.

"No one will want them," thought Diego.

As the day lengthened out into afternoon, the market place began to fill. Diego held out his pots with a bright smile, but the strangers passed them by. The small cactus plants in the ugly pots across the way drew the attention of the strangers.

"We are going to take them home and give them to our friends," the visitors pointed out. "Then they can see the kind of plants that grow in Cuba."

Once a northern lady stopped before Diego's pots and looked at them a little sadly. "If they only had something growing in them," she said, with regret, and walked on.

"They will surely not all like those ugly pots," Diego kept telling himself. "Some one will come to buy, then others will follow." One after the other came. They paused beside Diego's display for a moment. Then they moved on again.

When evening came, not a single one of Diego's pots had been sold. Unless he wished to give them away, he would have to take them on his head and walk home with them. Since he had no idea of giving away what he had spent many days in making, he gathered up his wares and set out for home.

Diego was very much ashamed of himself. His father had been a fine pottery maker, yet his son was so poor in his workmanship, he could not make a thing good enough to sell. "Perhaps the pots are a bit crooked around the edges," a voice within him whispered.

Diego walked on a bit farther, then he burst out, "No, my work is neither poor nor crooked! It is good."

He had not walked much farther when he met old Franco, who was on his way to town. He had a basket of fruit in either hand and a stack of hats on his head.

"You are going in the wrong direction," said he, so Diego had to tell him what had happened.

"Do not be so unhappy," Franco said before he continued on his way. "Every difficulty has two doors. One door leads in, so the other must lead out."

"It looks to me as though both doors lead in, and neither out," said Diego. But he felt a little happier now, and walked proudly again, the pots balanced easily on his head.

On and on he went. Before long he came to the pineapple field again. By this time he was so tired he sat down to rest. While sitting there he glanced down into the ditch beside the road. Some children had been playing there. It looked as though they had set up a store with boxes and empty cans. Into a tin can, half full of dirt, the top of a pineapple had either fallen or been planted. It had taken root and grown.

"It looks every bit as pretty as the cactus plants that man was selling in the market today," the boy told himself. With that he emptied the can into one of his pots. After he had filled the pot with dirt, he was surprised to see how splendid it looked.

"I shall plant bananas, sugar cane and pineapple in those clay pots of mine," said he. "Then people can really see what grows in this country of Cuba."

It took a few days before Diego could get his potted garden to thrive, but at last everything was ready, so the boy set out for the village again. This time, however, he did not carry the pots on his head. He took his mother's ox and the ox-cart.

Diego had not been in the market ten minutes before people from far and near gathered around.

"Won't you take one of these small pots of sugar cane with you?" he called in his high clear voice.

"Cuba is the principal sugar cane country in the world. Here is a pineapple plant and a small banana plant. Real Cuban plants in real Cuban pots!"

The strangers who had just arrived in the village crowded closely about the boy.

"We want to know more about bananas," they said. "If we took these plants home with us, could we make them grow into banana plants?"

"No," said Diego, "not unless you kept them in a greenhouse, for they need a great deal of heat."

"What kind of flower has the banana?"

"The blossom looks more like a bud than a flower. It is six inches long. Behind it, where the leaves join the trunk, is the cluster of green bananas. They grow with the fingers up instead of down, and there are over a hundred bananas on one stem."

The strangers wanted to know about the sugar cane, too. In less than half an hour Diego had sold every pot he had. Many people were standing by grumbling because there were no more for them.

That day as Diego rode home behind the old ox, he felt very happy and proud. As he passed the fields of sugar cane and pineapple, he bowed and said, "My friends, I think you will not see me so often after this, for I am going to be a pottery maker like my father. But now I do not hate you any more. You helped me when I was unhappy. Your little plants brought visitors to buy my pots. I will always think of you, and thank you, as I work at my wheel." Diego smiled and bowed again.

The sugar cane and the banana plants nodded back at him as though they had known all about it from the beginning.

THE BANANA CROP

Pedro lives in Colombia near the railway that winds its way from the inland points of Colombia north toward the harbor of Santa Marta. The train stops along the way to pick up bananas from small farms and from the large banana plantations. More than seven million stems of bananas were shipped from Colombia in one year.

Bananas are an important export of South and Central America and also an important food for the natives. The leaves of the banana plant are dried and used for roof coverings and for weaving baskets.

Only a single stem or bunch of bananas grows on each plant. After the stem is cut, the plant is cut low and produces another stem of bananas only after the stalk is full-grown again. The fruit is shipped green and ripens after it reaches its destination.

A KNIFE FOR PEDRO

BY THELMA GLAZER

"I wonder if it will come," sighed Pedro, "I wonder if it will ever come."

There on the side of the slope, he lay in the shade. Over his head the sun shone brightly on the tops of the tall coconut palm trees, as it does always in the morning on the hills of Colombia near the shores of the Caribbean Sea.

Pedro lay and dreamed, his bare brown feet cool against the moist ground, his head nestled snugly against his donkey's neck. Of all things in the world, Pedro loved best José, his thin donkey with straggly brown hair. José was named after a saint, just as Pedro was.

As they lay on the side of the steep hill, Pedro's eyes followed the straight rows of yams that he and his father had planted. Down at the end Pedro saw the tiny one-room hut that was his home. There it stood in the glaring light with its roof of dried leaves and straw to keep off the sun's heat, to hold the cool of the darkness inside. Out of the low, thatched hut came a thin twist of smoke. Pedro knew then that his mother was boiling bananas to serve on a palm leaf for breakfast.

Through the open doorway Pedro saw his fat brother, brown and naked, sitting on the earthen floor, sniffing the steam of boiling bananas. And all around him played the three shaggy dogs and a flock of white chickens.

Beyond the hut, at the end of the path, Pedro watched the tall heavy figure of his father. With his strong arms he steadied a large basket of yams on his head. Today he would carry them to his neighbor's hut.

Now Pedro felt hungry for breakfast. But he did not want to go home, for he was waiting for something. Both he and José were waiting. So Pedro reached into the thick foliage and picked a juicy mango. With his strong white teeth, he bit into the meaty softness of the fruit.

But all the while Pedro and José were listening for the sound they loved the best. Soon it came.

"It's here," shouted Pedro. "It's here at last!"

The long shrill whistle of the fruit train sounded in the distance. Pedro and José loved that piercing noise as it came nearer and nearer. First it filled the air with a sudden shriek, then slowly faded away, its sound lost in the hills. How they loved that far-off rumbling noise of the old rickety train, the rickety fruit train that takes bananas to the big boat that sails the Caribbean Sea to North America.

Pedro sighed. "Little José, every time I hear that long whistling call, I wish so hard that we could catch that train and sell the fruit merchant a bunch of bananas. Just think! He might give us a whole *peso*. Then we could take a long journey, you and I, to the village of Santa Marta. With that *peso*, I could buy something that I've wished for ever so long. I could buy a knife, a sharp knife with a strong wooden handle, one that I could call my very own."

Pedro sighed again and shook his head, sadly. He did not think his wish could come true.

Just then another sudden shriek of the train's whistle pierced the air. This time it seemed nearer than ever. It sounded so near that José jumped to his feet, pricked up his ears, and started sliding down the hillside.

"Come back, José, come back," called Pedro.

But down, down, along the straight rows of yams Pedro chased his donkey and caught him just under the banana tree that shaded the hut. But José yanked and pulled away from Pedro.

"Do you want to chase that whistle, little José?" Pedro stroked the dry straggly hair of his donkey. José pulled and yanked more and more.

Right at that moment, Pedro had an idea. He

decided to take a journey with José, to catch that fruit train. Perhaps, after all, he would be able to sell a bunch of bananas for a *peso*. But first he must cut the bananas.

Pedro found his father's precious knife, the only one that the whole family owned, and tied it to the end of a long wooden pole. He examined closely the four banana plants, each with its single stem, or bunch of green fruit. He chose the plant that bore a small but firm stem of unripe bananas.

Pedro reached up high and nicked the stalk of the plant carefully, only half-way through. Slowly, very slowly, with a crackling noise, the weight of the fruit bent the plant lower and lower. Carefully, Pedro caught the heavy bananas just before they touched the ground. Then, with a quick thrust of the knife, he cut the stem.

Patiently José stood near by, ready to be loaded for the journey. With a strong rope Pedro tied the stem of at least one hundred bananas to José's side. To balance the load for his little donkey, Pedro tied a load of papaya melons on the other side. They would do for eating on their journey.

Together they started off. All through the morning, with Pedro on his back, the little donkey trotted along the dry, dirt roads. The sun beat down with burning heat upon his thin straggly hair.

The dust blew up into his face, blinding his eyes. José's tongue was parched in his mouth. His legs felt tired and stiff under the weight of his heavy load. But on and on he trotted. The sun became hotter and hotter. The papayas and the bananas seemed heavier and heavier.

Suddenly, at a turn of the road, Pedro saw the shining railroad tracks and the little wayside shed that was the station. Then the long shrill whistle of the fruit train sounded again, coming nearer and nearer. Pedro kicked José hard with the heel of his bare foot.

"Hurry, hurry, José! We must reach that shed before the train passes by." Pedro yanked his donkey's straggly hair and tried to push him forward. But José's legs were very tired now and he went more and more slowly.

At last it happened, just as Pedro feared it might. The string of cars went rattling by, whirling past. They rumbled along on the silver tracks, far off into the distance, winding themselves in and out among the hills and finally curling around a bend out of sight. Too late! The train had gone.

The poor tired donkey sank down on the dry, hot road, and Pedro tumbled to the ground. The sun beat down with a glaring light, burning them with its fierce heat. There they squatted, a tired thirsty donkey with sad blurry eyes and an aching back; a weary boy with a heavy heart and a stem of one hundred useless bananas.

"Poor little José!" Pedro smoothed the dry scratchy side of his donkey. "All this way and all for nothing."

Sadly, Pedro untied one of the papaya melons and broke it open against his knee. The small brown seeds fell to the ground as he scooped them out with the tips of his fingers. Then he broke off a large piece of the fruit and pushed it into his donkey's mouth. José ate it eagerly, skin and all.

Then Pedro lay down, his hot body welcoming the cool of the prickly grass. He cupped a piece of melon in his hand and sucked out the rich juicy meat.

But all the while Pedro kept thinking of the fruit train, pushing and puffing in and out among the mountains, stopping here and there to pick up banana stems at the little wayside sheds. He could almost seem to hear it rumbling and rattling farther and farther away, twisting and winding on its path, along the trail of the Magdalena River. On and on it would go until it reached the port of Santa Marta on the Caribbean Sea.

No! There was nothing else to do but to rest for a little while in the cool shade with his donkey. Then they would have to start on the hot journey home, but without the *peso,* without the knife.

Pedro closed his eyes and was soon almost asleep. Suddenly he was surprised by that same piercing sound, shooting through the air, shrieking from the far hills. With a startled leap, José rushed toward the railroad tracks. Pedro ran after him.

"Come back, little José, come back," he called. "You cannot catch that train!"

But the donkey raced on and on, his thin straggly hair sticking out on his dry skin, his load of bananas and papaya melons bobbing up and down as he ran. In the broiling heat, on the dusty road, Pedro chased after his donkey.

Finally, Pedro caught up with José and grabbed him by the ears. José still pulled and pulled in the direction of the train. Pedro tried to hold him back, but the donkey pulled harder and harder.

"Foolish little José, so you want to catch that train!" Pedro thought for a while. Then why not let him? They were only a day's journey from the port of Santa Marta. Perhaps they could reach the dock before the boat sailed. Pedro knew that beginning with sunset, all night long and all through the next morning, the strong brown men who worked on the dock would unload thousands of banana stems from the train. They would load them on a moving belt that would take them down into the hold of the big boat. Then the boat would sail across the Caribbean Sea to carry the fruit far, far away to North America.

Pedro made up his mind quickly. José wanted to go and he wanted to go. The road was long and the sun was hot, but he did not want to waste a whole stem of bananas.

So Pedro turned the donkey down the road that followed the tracks. It was a dirty, bumpy road that stretched on and on for many miles, along the shore of the Magdalena River. All through the scorching heat of the day and all through the blinding dust, he trotted.

After a long, long weary time, Pedro saw the red ball of the setting sun sink low in the sky. The evening wind felt cold on Pedro's back and buzzed sharply against his ears.

Poor little José! His knees ached with soreness and his eyes were half closed. But on and on, as the sunset glow faded, he dragged his heavy load.

All the while, Pedro kept repeating, "Just a little further, José, and we'll be there."

Finally, they came around a turn in the road, and saw in the distance the broad calm surface of the sea. They knew then that they were near the end of their long journey. Pedro forgot the chill of the cold wind on his back. He forgot the tired feeling in his bones. And the donkey, sniffing the freshness of the sea air, quickened the rhythm of his stiff legs.

At last José reached the crowded dock. His legs caved in under him. He sank down completely exhausted. Pedro, straining his tired arms to lift the heavy stem of bananas, poised them on the top of his head. He pushed his way through the noisy

crowd to find the fruit merchant who sat on a high wooden chair near the train. All around him sounded the cries of many voices:

"Parrots for sale!"

"Buy my boxes of carved stained wood!"

"Buy a little donkey!"

Pedro stopped short suddenly. He saw something that made his heart sink. There on the dock lay hundreds of banana stems piled higher than his head. Surely the merchant would not choose Pedro's bananas when he had refused all these others!

But Pedro and José had journeyed far from

home. They had suffered from heat and thirst. Even more than before, Pedro was determined to earn a *peso* and to buy a knife.

So Pedro carried the heavy stem of bananas to the merchant. Timidly he reached up and pulled the edge of the man's sleeve.

"*Señor,* if you please?"

The fruit buyer took a quick look at Pedro's bananas. Then he looked again, more carefully.

"That's the kind of a stem we like," he said finally. "They are unripe and firm and have no black spots!"

Quickly he dug into his pockets, pulled out a *peso* and put it into Pedro's brown palm.

"*Gracias, señor,*" murmured Pedro.

He dragged his tired feet back through the crowds on the dock to the side of his donkey.

"We have the *peso,* little José," he said, patting the donkey's dusty sides. "We have the *peso* at last."

What matter now if their bodies were sore from the long, long journey? What matter if their throats were dry with dust and thirst? They were ever so tired but it did not matter. Now they had sold their stem of bananas and had earned a *peso*.

So Pedro and José found a quiet spot behind one of the long string of cars. The donkey lay down and Pedro curled up beside him. The hand in his pocket clutched the *peso*. In the morning, on their journey home, he would buy a knife, a sharp knife, that he could call his very own.

Pedro and José soon fell fast asleep. They slept all through the night near the rickety, rumbly train that carries bananas to the big boat that sails the Caribbean Sea to North America.

EXPORTING BALSAM SAP

Pepito lives in El Salvador along the narrow strip of coast land where balsam-of-Peru trees grow. The natives gather the sap from the trees and send it to Bebedero, a little railroad town near the edge of the forests. From there, most of the sap is shipped to the United States.

The sap is used for many different purposes in this country. It is very valuable in treating bronchial diseases. It is used in salves, pomades, perfumes and confections.

Although the trees grow in Central America, they are called balsam-of-Peru trees because the sap used to be shipped from Peru. The Spanish conquerors found Indians using it four hundred years ago. They sent some of it back to the Old World and ever since then it has been gathered and exported.

YOUNG BALSAMERO

BY E. MARK PHILLIPS

When Pepito opened his eyes that morning, he knew something was wrong. Kicking off his thin blanket, he sat up on his bed mat. The hut was unusually quiet. Where were his grandmother and grandfather?

The outside door was open. Through it came a faint sweet smell of vanilla. But that was not unusual. The two-roomed hut where he and his grandparents lived was near the great balsam-of-Peru forests. In their yard grew their own balsam trees from which they made their living. And the balsam-of-Peru tree always gives off the odor of vanilla.

Pepito did not live in the country named Peru. He lived on the balsam coast of El Salvador, the only place in the world where there is a balsam-of-Peru forest.

Pepito sat watching the big square of sunshine on the floor. The floor was made of a rich, reddish black wood, almost as hard as ivory, and polished to a satiny glow. It was made of a balsam-of-Peru tree that had grown too old to give off any sap. The sunshine was picking out all the red in the hard wood, making it shine and sparkle. It was beautiful. Pepito loved to watch it. Suddenly, it reminded him of what was wrong.

It was not raining. It had not rained for three days. Two nights ago they had seen the new moon. It was time for the *balsameros* to begin gathering the sap. Today his grandfather was to cut the windows in the bark of their own trees.

His grandfather was one of the best *balsameros* in all the balsam coast. When he was younger and stronger, the men who owned the trees in the forest used to hire him to gather their sap. Pepito wanted to be a good *balsamero,* too.

He sprang up and ran to the curtained doorway between the big room and the small one with the fireplace where they cooked and ate their meals. Since he slept in the few clothes he wore during the day, he did not have to stop to dress.

He jerked the curtain aside. His grandfather sat huddled in a blanket on the bench beside the fireplace. His grandmother stood beside him, a worried look on her face.

"Grandfather!" he cried, running to him. "What is it?" But he knew. His grandfather was sick.

The first new moon of the summer had come. It was time for all *balsameros* to be making the *ventanas*, or windows, in their trees if they would not lose any precious sap. And now his grandfather was sick.

They were alone. Not until the *balsameros* who lived much farther up the coast came by on the way to the market with their trees' first flow of sap would they see any friends. What would they do? Without the money for their balsam sap, how could they live?

"What shall we do, Grandmother?" Pepito whispered.

"You must catch one of the donkeys and go to Bebedero. The good *Señor* Felipe, the merchant, will let you stay the night at his house. Tell him your grandfather is sick and ask him to find a *balsamero* to come gather our sap."

Bebedero was the little station on the railroad where most of the sap from the forest was sold to the balsam merchants. It was over a half day's ride away, along the cart road. Pepito had thought it would be a proud day in his life when he could go there alone. Now, he did not want to go.

"Oh, Grandmother," he begged, "let me gather the sap. For a long time, Grandfather has let me help him. And last year he even let me cut one of the *ventanas*. Please, Grandmother, I'm past ten and not small for my age."

"But you are so young to be a *balsamero*, Pepito. We must have all the sap our trees will give, and some of it soon. Our food is almost gone."

"But if you hire a *balsamero* you will have to give him almost half of our sap," Pepito replied.

"I know," Grandmother said sadly, "but there seems no other way."

"Just let me try, Grandmother."

She looked across the yard at their trees. There were twelve of them. The oldest and biggest of all was the one Grandfather's own grandfather had set out. It was almost a hundred years old now. Soon it would give no more sap. The youngest was the slender shoot that Pepito had set out just last year. Pepito would be a man long before its *ventana* could be cut. They all loved their trees, and no one loved them more than Pepito did. Not for worlds would he harm one of them.

"Let me do one of them," he said eagerly. "If it is not done right, then I will go for a real *balsamero.*"

"You are a good *chico*. You may try one tree." Tears came into her eyes. "Now eat your *tortillas*. I will go to give your grandfather the herbs I have brewed for him and get him to his bed again."

Presently she brought Pepito the short-handled mallet with the head of smooth hard wood for bruising the bark, and the *machete,* a sharp-bladed knife for cutting.

They went first to the old tree. Pepito walked slowly around the great trunk with its roots spreading out over the ground. All over the bark were the healed or healing scars where other *ventanas* had been cut. It takes three or four years for a scar to heal, and Pepito knew that a good *balsamero* never cuts into an unhealed scar.

"I'll make the window here," he said finally, and put his *machete* on the ground. He took the mallet handle in both hands and began tapping, carefully, steadily, just as his grandfather had taught him.

Tap-tap-tap, went the wooden mallet. Tap-tap-tap-tap. He must strike just hard enough to loosen the outer bark.

Pepito made a straight line of bruises almost all the way around the tree. Then he made another line just under that, and another, and another. At last he had tapped out a rectangle on the bark. It was as wide as his mallet was long, which was the way his grandfather measured.

In the back, Pepito left a wide strip of bark untouched. This piece of bark was called the life of the tree. If the tree were bruised all the way around it might die. Now that the tapping was finished, the cutting came next.

He put the sharp edge of the knife on the upper side of the rectangle. His face pale, his hands cold

but steady, he pressed down until he felt the blade sink through the outer bark. Slowly, around the whole rectangle, the big knife went.

Two or three times Pepito felt it sink too deeply in and lifted it quickly. With the blade he lifted a corner of the bark. Then, dropping the knife, he took hold with both hands and pulled back with all his might. There was a ripping, sucking noise and the whole rectangle of bark was off. He had made the *ventana*.

His grandmother leaned close to look at the bare wood. Only a few cuts and they were not deep ones.

"*Bueno,*" she said, "very good. Now rest."

She went back into the hut, and Pepito knew that he could go on. Although there were only seven of the trees old enough to be giving sap, the long day was ended before Pepito had cut his last *ventana.* Now they must wait for the sap to begin its full flow. It was hard work being a *balsamero,* but who would want to be anything else, Pepito wondered.

Every day after that, Pepito went into the forest to gather fresh herbs that his grandmother wanted to brew for his grandfather. He brought wood for the cooking fire, and kept watch to see that their two donkeys did not stray too far away.

He kept a close watch on the balsam trees, too. Early on the sixth morning after the *ventanas* had been cut, he smelled not a faint odor of vanilla but a strong one.

The *ventanas* were all covered with dark drops oozing out of the wood.

"Grandmother!" he cried. "The sap! The sap is running!"

Soon, Grandmother came hurrying out with the *trapos,* long strips of clean white cloth. These must be bound around the tree trunks where the *ventanas* had been cut, so that not a drop of the precious sap would be lost.

The weather stayed warm and sunny. The sap flowed freely. And, little by little, Grandfather grew better.

In ten days the *trapos* were damp and heavy with the thick sap. Pepito and his grandmother set up the biggest iron kettle on two rocks near the hut, filled it half full of water and built a fire under it. When the water boiled, they took the *trapos* from the trees and put them into it.

The sweet-smelling, gummy sap melted away from the *trapos* in the hot water. Then the *trapos* were put into the squeezing net. The net was made so that two people, without burning their hands, could squeeze back into the kettle the last drop of sap left in the cloths.

After this, the sap and the water must boil for half an hour, while some one kept stirring it with a long paddle to make sure it did not boil over.

When the sap had boiled for half an hour, the fire would be put out. As it cooled, the heavy sap would sink to the bottom, and the water and pieces of bark or dirt would rise to the top. When all the sap had settled, then the water would be poured off and the heavy mass of sweet-smelling balsam would be dipped into the waiting, earthen jar. It would be beautiful then, like pale, clear amber. As they worked, the air around them became heavier and heavier with the odor.

It was while Pepito stirred the bubbling kettle with the long paddle, his face red from the fire, that they heard a noise at the open door of the hut.

"It's Grandfather!" Pepito shouted, but he dared not stop stirring the boiling kettle.

Grandmother hurried to help the sick man onto the bench by the doorway. She pulled a thin blanket over his knees and scolded him for coming outside alone. Then she brought him a bowl of bean soup, thick soup this time, that she had just made. But he could drink only a few swallows.

Grandfather had said no word. He had looked at Pepito, smiling at him as he stirred the kettle. He had looked long at the trees with their *ventanas* waiting for fresh *trapos*. His eyes seemed to be seeking something else. Finally he spoke, in a weak voice. "Where is the *balsamero?*"

"Pepito," Grandmother told him. "Our little Pepito. And not a single tree is damaged."

It seemed that Grandfather could not quite believe it. He passed a shaking hand across his eyes, looked again at his beloved trees and looked again at Pepito.

"Pepito?" he whispered.

Grandmother nodded. "Within a few days some of our *balsamero* friends will pass on their way to Bebedero. They can take our first balsam and bring back the food we need."

Grandfather reached down and, with an effort,

picked up the bowl of soup. His voice seemed stronger when he spoke.

"No," he said. "Pepito must be ready to go with them. A real *balsamero* takes his own balsam to market."

And Pepito, although he was bursting with pride and happiness, kept right on stirring the bubbling sweet-smelling kettle.

GLOSSARY

All Spanish words are marked Sp.

balsam—a gumlike sap of fragrant odor coming from certain plants and trees.
balsamero (bahl-sah-may'-ro)—man whose trade is to gather sap from the balsam-of-Peru tree.
Bebedero (beh-beh-day'-ro) Sp.—the name of a village in El Salvador which is a shipping point for sap.
bueno (bway'-no) Sp.—good.
cactus—plants with fleshy stems and branches that bear scales or prickles instead of leaves.
Caribbean (car-i-bee'-an)—an arm of the Atlantic Ocean between the West Indies and South America.
chico (chee'-ko) Sp.—little, often used in speaking to a child.
Diego (dee-ay'-go) Sp.—James.
Felipe (feh-lee'-pay) Sp.—Philip.
gourd (gored)—the fruit of a vine related to the pumpkin and melon. Its dried shell is often used as a dipper.
gracias (grah'-see-ahs) Sp.—thank you.
José (hoe-say') Sp.—Joseph.
machete (mah-chay'-tay) Sp.—a large knife used

for cutting banana stems and sugar cane and for doing other heavy work.

Magdalena (mahg-dah-lay'-na)—the principal river of Colombia, on which much of the produce of the interior is shipped to the coast.

mango—a tropical fruit, reddish in color, good to eat.

papaya (pah-pah'-ya)—the pulpy yellow fruit of a tropical American tree.

Pedro (pay'-dro) Sp.—Peter.

Pepito (peh-pee'-toe) Sp.—little Joe, a short form of Pepe, or Joe.

peso (pay'-so) Sp.—a unit of money corresponding in general to our dollar, though its value changes.

plantain—a kind of large banana that is cooked and eaten as a vegetable.

Santa Marta—a seaport on the coast of Colombia.

señor (sane-yore') Sp.—Mr. or sir.

tortillas (tore-tea'-yas) Sp.—thin, flabby cakes, something like pancakes but made of corn.

trapos (trah'-pos) Sp.—literally, rags. In this story used to mean the strips of cloth wrapped around the tree to catch the sap.

ventanas (ven-tah'-nahs) Sp.—windows, or openings.

yams—a root vegetable which takes the place of the potato in the West Indies and elsewhere.

NORMANDALE COMMUNITY COLLEGE
LIBRARY
9700 FRANCE AVENUE SOUTH
BLOOMINGTON, MN 55431-4399

Printed in the United States
25088LVS00001B/275